I0782115

FEEL

Northern State Hospital

mark favero

Broken Locks

You Will Be Mine

Decaying Actualities

Northern State Hospital

"Decaying Actualities" is more than a visual journey; it's an emotional and historical exploration. It reminds us of when those with mental disorders were often outcasts confined to institutions like the Northern State Hospital. Some may argue that those days are behind us, but the relics of the past combined with contemporary attitudes towards mental health paint a different picture. While the walls of such institutions may crumble, have the walls we've built around understanding and addressing mental illness indeed come down?

With this collection, I invite you to observe and feel—to immerse yourself in the intersection of past and present, man and nature, neglect and hope. In these decaying actualities lie stories that need to be told, lessons to be learned, and a call for change. As you navigate this collection, may you be moved to introspection, empathy, and action, ensuring that the decay of the past is not repeated in the future.

Distant Existence

Losing The Path

Neglected Dreams

Day Room Echoes

These shattered windows reflect a fragmented understanding of mental health. It is time to rebuild with compassion and clarity rather than fear.

Silently Failing

Empty Pathways

These peeling walls witnessed countless stories, silenced by neglect and shame. The silence lingers, urging us to break the cycle of dismissal and stigma.

Forgotten Wards

Lost Sanctuary

Daytime Whispers

Now rusted and broken, the barred windows speak of isolation's grip. They remind us of the walls that still separate those struggling from the compassion they deserve.

Waiting for Reality

Fragments of the Past

A Journey

Crumbling Memories

Hall of Echoes

Veiled in Debris

Alone In My Room

And I Wait

Each crumbling brick reflects a life confined, an echo of misunderstood humanity. The decay reveals a history of isolation born from fear rather than understanding.

Blurred Realities

Shadows of the Past

Taking Back

Nature's slow reclamation of this place mirrors the forgotten stories beneath. As vines entwine, they remind us of the delicate balance between neglect and rebirth.

Peeling Back Memories

Each Room A Story

The empty halls echo not only with absence but also with opportunity lost. The lives left behind are a call to nurture those we have historically ignored.

Forward or Backward

Split Realities

What remains is not just a building but a testament to our failure to see humanity. We must learn to see beyond the illness and recognize the person within.

Blind Eye

Walking to the....

This decay is the physical manifestation of our disregard for the human spirit. Yet even in decay, the possibility of renewal remains—if we are willing to change.

Frozen in the past

Lost Support

Rotted to the core

The decay may be inevitable for these walls, but for our empathy, it does not have to be. The past serves as a warning: let us not abandon hope for the living.

Weathering

Failing in Time

Every rusted hinge, every broken door tells of lives left on the fringes. It is time to bring these stories back into the center of our understanding.

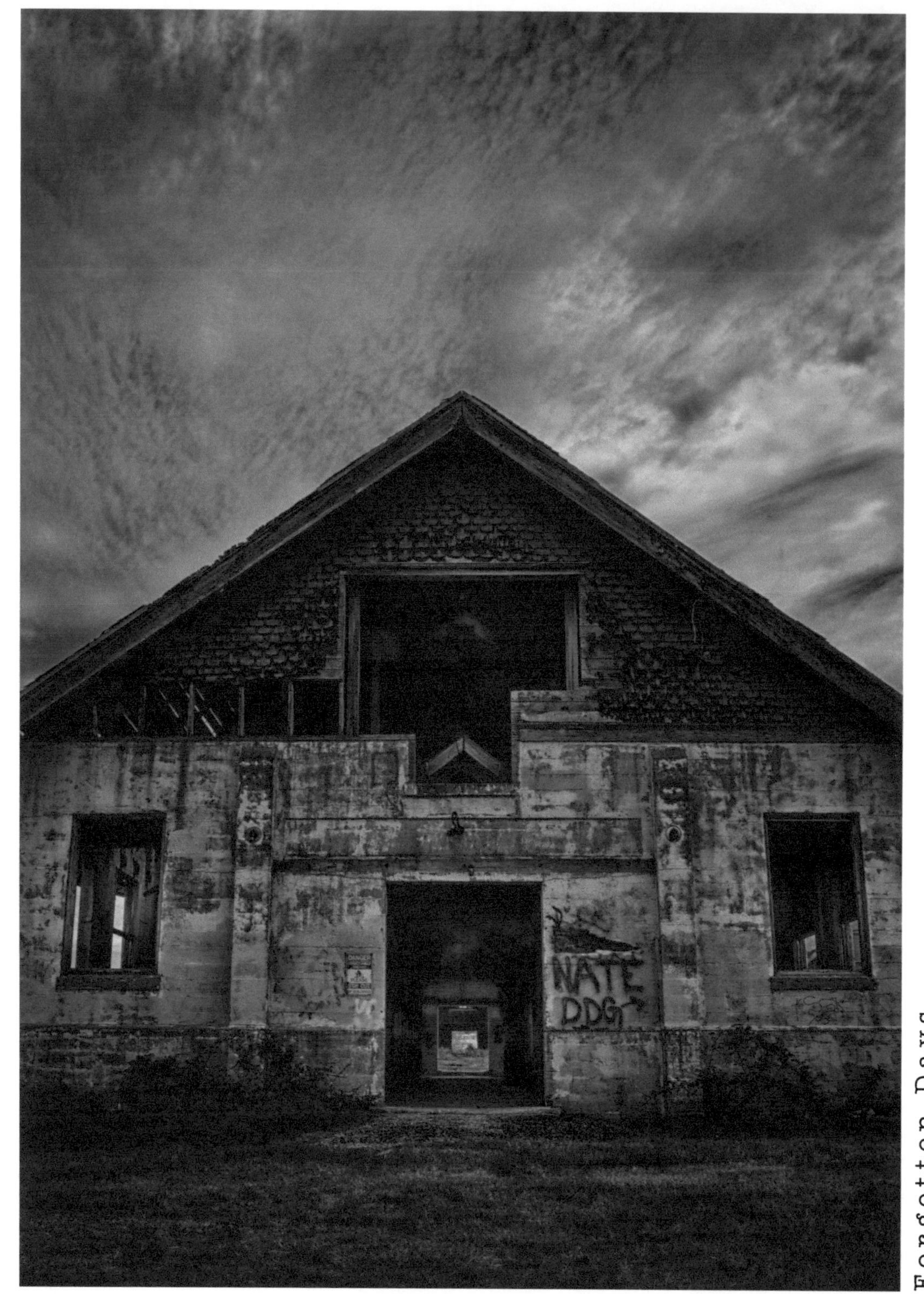

Forgotten Days

Passage in Ruins

Collapsing Under

Beaten by Man and Time

The rusting locks symbolize how we have kept hope and understanding confined. Actual progress requires us to open doors, not seal them shut in fear.

Sealed from View

Reclaiming the Past

Tentacles of Vine

Overgrown grounds remind us that time waits for no one. If we do not nurture those in need, nature and neglect will overtake what could have been saved.

Swallowed by Nature

As we reach the end of "Decaying Actualities," I invite you to linger with the images and allow them to speak to you in their way. These scenes of decay and reclamation hold stories that go beyond the surface—stories of human experience, forgotten histories, and echoes that still resonate today. Let these visuals stir your thoughts about the intersection of past and present, neglect and care, and what it means to support one another truly.

May these images prompt you to explore what has been lost and what we might still have the power to change.

Fading to the Past

Copyright 2024 - All Rights Reserved
Mark Favero
Feel - Northern State Hospital
Decaying Actualities
www.markfaverophoto.com